Technically,
It's Not My Fault

W9-CBA-679

Technically, It's Not My Fault

Concrete Poems by John Grandits

Clarion Books   New York

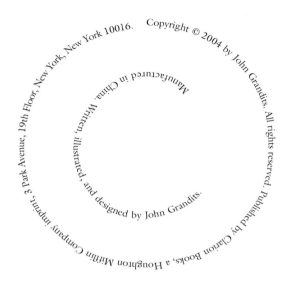

3 Park Avenue, 19th Floor, New York, New York 10016. Copyright © 2004 by John Grandits. All rights reserved. Published by Clarion Books, a Houghton Mifflin Company imprint. Manufactured in China. Written, illustrated, and designed by John Grandits.

For information about permission to reproduce selections from this book, write to trade.permissions@hmhco.com or to Permissions, Houghton Mifflin Harcourt Publishing Company, 3 Park Avenue, 19th Floor, New York, New York 10016.

www.hmhco.com

Library of Congress Cataloging-in-Publication Data
Grandits, John.
Technically, it's not my fault : concrete poems / by John Grandits
p. cm.
CL ISBN 0-618-42833-X
PA ISBN 0-618-50361-7
1. Concrete poetry, American. 2. Children's poetry, American. I Title
PS3607.R363B73 2004
811'.6—dc22   2004000231

CL ISBN-13: 978-0-618-42833-5
CL ISBN-10: 0-618-42833-X

PA ISBN-13: 978-0-618-50361-2
PA ISBN-10: 0-618-50361-7

SCP   25 24 23 22 21 20
4500754543
Printed in China

Thanks to Mom and James and Andrea and Marcia and Dinah and Ranney Matt and Bagel Joe and Elm Place Lillian and Stellar Linda and Skateboard Communist.

For
Joanne & Jordan

MY STUPID DAY

I wake up in the morning and get ready for school. It's the same thing every day. I go to school and it's BORING. I have lunch and talk to the same kids day after day. When I get home, I have the same stupid snack and watch a dumb cartoon. Then it's dinner and homework and the day is over. So I put on my pajamas. I go to bed, and then

MY
SISTER
IS CRAZY

My sister wears a
pyramid on her head.
That's right. She has a
little pyramid-shaped hat.
"What is wrong with you?"
I ask her. "You look like a jerk!"
My sister sighs and rolls her eyes,
as if I'm the one who's a total loon.

"The pyramid is a source of ancient power,"
she says. "The Egyptians had pyramids, and
their empire lasted 3,000 years. The Aztecs ruled
Mexico with an iron fist. Or was it the Incas? No, Aztecs,
I think. Anyway, they had pyramids. And how about the
pyramid on the one-dollar bill? Coincidence? I don't think so."

My sister is crazy. That's because she's getting bombarded by alien
anti-brain waves from outer space. Super-intelligent beings from the
Nebula Galaxy are shooting at us with pluton rays that can make you
go crazy. They're not aiming at everyone, of course. Just my family.

That's why I wear aluminum foil on my head. I have a very good looking
ray-deflecting foil hat that I made myself. Not in the shape of a pyramid!
You'd have to be nuts to think that a pyramid would protect your brain from
evil alien rays coming from outer space. Which proves my point: My sister is crazy.

The Thank-You Letter[1]

Dear Aunt Hildegard,

Thank you[2] for the amazing gifts.[3] It was terrific[4] getting your package![5] I grabbed it immediately.[6] But when my parents saw it,[7] they said[8] I shouldn't open it until my birthday. You can imagine how I felt when I found two gifts![9] The sweater was totally awesome.[10] It's amazing how well you know me.[11]

Then there was the poster you got for my room.[12] You're in luck; I don't already have a Polka Hall of Fame poster.[13] I'm putting it right under my World Wrestling Federation poster.[14]

Thanks,[15] thanks,[16] and thanks again.[17] I'm already planning when to wear my new sweater.[18]

Your 11-year-old[19] nephew,

Robert

1. with Footnotes

2. For nothing!

3. Do you have the slightest clue what an 11-year-old boy likes?

4. I almost croaked when I saw the package. I still remember last year's gift. "Oh, no! Not again!" I screamed.

5. I was in luck. Mom didn't see the mailman.

6. I hid the package in the garage under the hose.

7. What were the chances that Dad would decide to wash the car *that* day?

8. "What's this?" they said. "When did this come?"

9. You monster.

10. In the history of sweaters, there has never been an uglier waste of yarn.

11. Where did you *ever* find a sweater that not only has Barney on it but also is two sizes too big for me?

12. I'm old enough to decorate my own room.

13. Just what I need—a picture of an old guy with an accordion.

14. And I do mean UNDER.

15. For trying to embarrass me in front of my friends.

16. For the lectures from my parents.

17. For making me waste an hour of my life writing this stupid thank-you letter.

18. I know they'll make me wear it the next time you come to visit. I just hope nobody sees me.

19. I'm 11!!! Get it?!?

TyrannosaurBus Rex

I am the vicious TyrannosaurBus Rex.
I roam the suburbs, hunting.
Those who see me gaze in terror.
Those who are spared are grateful.

Early in the morning, I spy
a group of small human children
standing on the corner of Elm and Spring.
I slam on my brakes.
I open my mouth.
"Come in, little children," I say.
They don't want to, but they must.
Their parents have delivered them to me.
Human sacrifices.

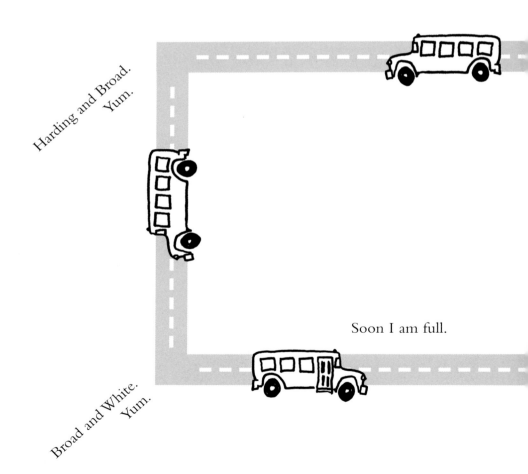

Harding and Broad.
Yum.

Soon I am full.

Broad and White.
Yum.

I eat the humans.
They are young and tender.
Yum.

Then I go to Elm and Hudson.
More children. More sacrifices.
Yum.

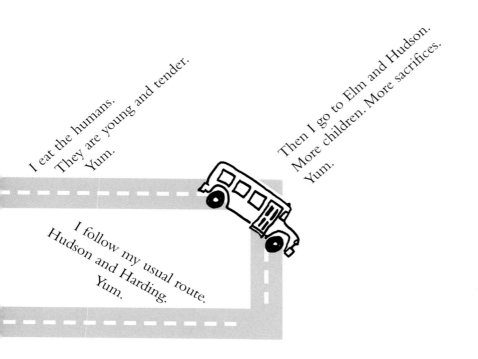

I follow my usual route.
Hudson and Harding.
Yum.

My breakfast is noisy.
My breakfast is jumping around in my stomach.
My breakfast is giggling and laughing and arguing.
My stomach is queasy.
I don't feel so good.

I go to the
school parking lot.
I open my mouth
and barf out my noisy,
jumping,
giggling,
laughing,
arguing
breakfast.

next to the school and hunt again.
when I will go to the parking lot
and dream dreams about 3:30,
from hunting, I settle into my nap
I'm so tired

The Australian Cane Toad

The cane toad does not belong in Australia.
He doesn't like it much.
"How did I get here?" he asks himself.
"These Australian bugs taste awful."
Unfortunately for the toad, a dingo sneaks up from behind.
Snap! Crunch! Gulp! . . . Ahhh.
Unfortunately for the dingo, the cane toad is poisonous.
Very poisonous.

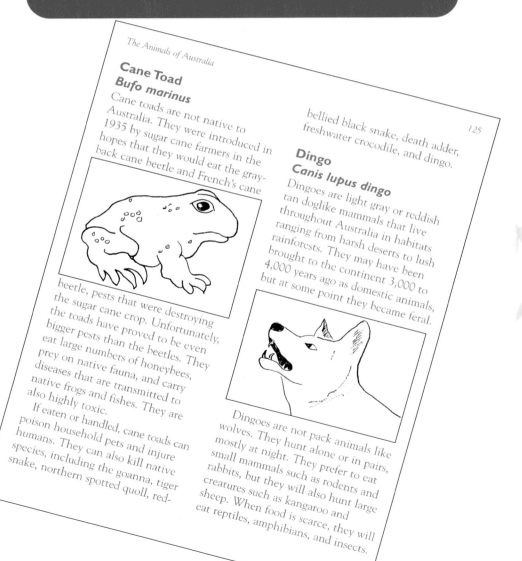

The Animals of Australia

Cane Toad
Bufo marinus

Cane toads are not native to Australia. They were introduced in 1935 by sugar cane farmers in the hopes that they would eat the gray-back cane beetle and French's cane beetle, pests that were destroying the sugar cane crop. Unfortunately, the toads have proved to be even bigger pests than the beetles. They eat large numbers of honeybees, prey on native fauna, and carry diseases that are transmitted to native frogs and fishes. They are also highly toxic.

If eaten or handled, cane toads can poison household pets and injure humans. They can also kill native species, including the goanna, tiger snake, northern spotted quoll, red-bellied black snake, death adder, freshwater crocodile, and dingo.

125

Dingo
Canis lupus dingo

Dingoes are light gray or reddish tan doglike mammals that live throughout Australia in habitats ranging from harsh deserts to lush rainforests. They may have been brought to the continent 3,000 to 4,000 years ago as domestic animals, but at some point they became feral.

Dingoes are not pack animals like wolves. They hunt alone or in pairs, mostly at night. They prefer to eat small mammals such as rodents and rabbits, but they will also hunt large creatures such as kangaroo and sheep. When food is scarce, they will eat reptiles, amphibians, and insects.

I'm supposed to be doing my science homework.
But really I'm reading about the cane toad.
The homework sheet is about magnets.
It's stupid. Not only stupid, but easy.
We had all this stuff last year.
The teacher must think we're morons.
Well, some of us *are* morons,
so she's partially right.
It's just that *I'm* not a moron.
Multiple choice:

> ☐ One answer is right.
> ☐ Two are close if you're not
>   paying attention.
> ☐ One is wrong.
> ☐ And one is you-must-not-
>   have-the-brains-God-gave-
>   a-chicken wrong.

I answer each question with the
chicken-brain option.

Worksheet # 4 -- Magnets

Name **Robert**

Room **107**

Now that you've read about magnet
experiments, answer the following

1. Magnets will attract:
   ☐ Anything metal
   ☐ Anything really hard
   ☐ Aluminum
   ☑ Wood
   ☐ Attention
2. A magnet has two poles called:
   ☐ Big and little
   ☑ North and South
   ☐ Homer and Marge
   ☐ Pushy and pully
   ☐ Positive up and positive down
3. A magnetic field is:
   ☐ the area affected by the pull of
   ☑ a place to grow magnet bushes
   ☐ copper wire wrapped around a magne
   ☐ the speed of electricity
   ☐ the area of a triangle

On the school bus the next day,
I run into Ronald Workman.
Ronald is big.
Really big.
And dumb, with a brain the size of a—oh,
I don't know, maybe a chicken's.
He's the seventh-grade equivalent of a Triceratops.
Except carnivorous.
"Hey, dweeb. Give me your science homework," he says.
"I don't think that would be a good idea," I croak.
But it's difficult to explain why because of the headlock.
"I think it's a good idea," Ronald cleverly answers.
"What are you going to do about it, anyway?"
Unfortunately for the Triceratops, the homework is poisonous.
Very poisonous.

SKATEBOARD

I'm on my totally cool new board and I'm *bombing the hill.* I do a little cut jump up a curb into the

I do a little cut jump up a

lift onto the bench,

Out of the lot, curb, across the street, curb, into the park. I do a sweet little

Busted. Walking home. I'm a sad old dog who's been swatted with a rolled-up newspaper.

7-Eleven parking lot and try a tight little figure eight just to see how she corners, and I'm about to try a tricky little ollie over a milk crate when all of a sudden I hear HEY, KID! No skateboards in the parking lot. Get outta here!

land clean, p-u-u-u-m-p up the hill, around the flagpole, d-o-o-o-w-n the ramp, and HEY, YOU! Can't you read the sign? No skateboarding!

I give up. I'm just gonna

veg in front of the TV and not think about it.

I mean, why bother, and then HEY, What are you doing inside? You begged for that skateboard, Robert. Now go out and use it!

DRAWKCAB

Mrs. Kosacowski started it.
Last week in social studies class she said to me,
"Robert, sometimes I think you're brilliant,
and other times I think you're absolutely backward,
and that you act backward on purpose."

So I'm teaching myself
to be backward on purpose.

Today Mrs. K. asked,
"Robert, are you paying attention?"
"On, ton yllaer," I answered.
"What did you say?" she said.
"I ma gniklat drawkcab yadot," I explained.
"Oh, my goodness. Are you having a seizure?"
Mrs. K. looked a little worried.
"On, I ma enif." I tried to reassure her. "Tub ouy
thgim eb gninrael-deriapmi."
She sent me to the nurse's office.

"I ma yllaer yako," I told the nurse.
She called my mom anyway.
Mom will have to take off from work
to come pick me up.
But I'm not worried.
I can explain everything.
I just hope Mom understands drawkcab klat.

What Are You Thinking About, Robert?

My gym clothes weren't THAT bad. It's only been six weeks. You could still tell what color they were.

Marcia Feddleston came over to talk to me in the hall.

Another unit on Sacajawea?! Can't they find a different girl hero to bore us with?

WWE Smackdown is on at 11:00 tonight, but I'm supposed to be in bed at 10:30.

Why don't they make scratch-and-sniff fart stickers?

Dickie Erickson says, "Marcia Feddleston likes you." So I say, "So what?" "Not that kind of likes you. I mean planning-the-honeymoon likes you."

Ronald Wotkman was showing off a pack of cigarettes in the boys' bathroom. What an idiot. Hope he gets caught.

I'm a good person. Why shouldn't she like me?

And he goes, "Not that like me?"

I don't care HOW hungry I am, I hate cucumbers, and I'm not eating them.

No time for breakfast. Forgot my lunch. Only had 45 cents. Man, am I hungry.

Got up late.

Nothin'.

"Robert, it's your turn to let Chips out!"
"Okay, okay. I'm going.

"Where is that dog?"

Hey!

TRIP

Ooops

BANG

Ayee!

Yiiiii

**ON THE STAIRS
IN THE MIDDLE
OF THE NIGHT**

THUD

SMASH

Ouch!

Oooof

SPLAT

FLIP

F L O P

"Stupid dog."

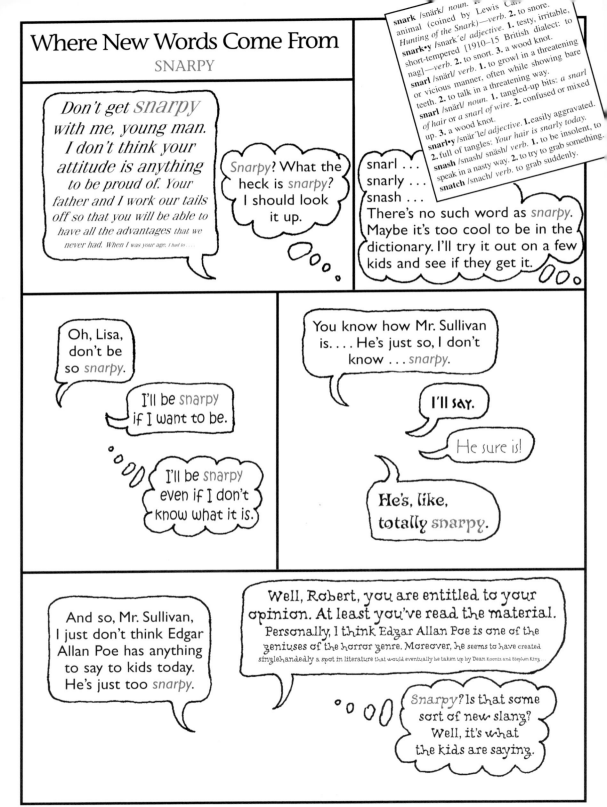

So when I was talking to my class today, I told them that they really had to have more respect for their teachers. Respect for the authority figure is what western civilization is built on. But I tried to put it to them in their own language. "Don't get *snarpy* with The Man," I said.

Oh, Bill, you are so hip! The kids must *LOVE* you.

What the heck is he talking about now?

My boyfriend, Bill, teaches seventh grade and he can't seem to leave his work at school. He's so-o-o-o juvenile. I think I've got to dump him. He's too *snarpy*.

So he's a little *snarpy*! So what! Don't be so picky.

Today on the Style Network: What's in? What's out? How do we know what the beautiful people are saying? Who decides what's hip? We go to our trend correspondent, Marsala Piquet. Marsala?

Thanks, Morton. In the past, when an older man—like yourself—said or did something new, it became fashion. Nowadays younger and younger kids are deciding what's hip and what's not, what's in and what's out. Fashion is made in middle school or even grammar school. Clothes, language, hair color, even what we eat and drink are determined by kids. But don't worry, Morton, we still think you're very *snarpy*! Back to you.

The president announced today that the country of Bizaristan faces strict censure and loss of trading privileges with the U.S. if it doesn't alter its foreign policy. CNN has this exclusive interview. . . . Mr. President, could you tell the American people -- what *is* the problem in Bizaristan?

In a nutshell, Wolf, it's their attitude. In the White House, we think they're a 10 on the *Snarpy*-Attitude Scale. If we don't address these issues now, the American people will suffer in the long run. That's why I am sending the secretary of state . . .

Wow! I guess *snarpy* really *is* a word.

THE TOWER

hair hair hair hair hair hair
hair hair hair hair hair hair
hair hair hair hair hair hair

Rapunzel, Rapunzel, let down your hair, I said. And she did. I started climbing. Watch out for my hair, she said, I don't want split ends. Take your boots off, I just washed it, she said. Watch out for my barrette, it's my favorite! she said. Why are you slowing down? Aren't you strong enough to rescue me? Why did you stop? What kind of prince are you, anyway? I climbed back down. I've heard about this other princess who's asleep—a real beauty.

How We Ended Up with a Plain Pizza

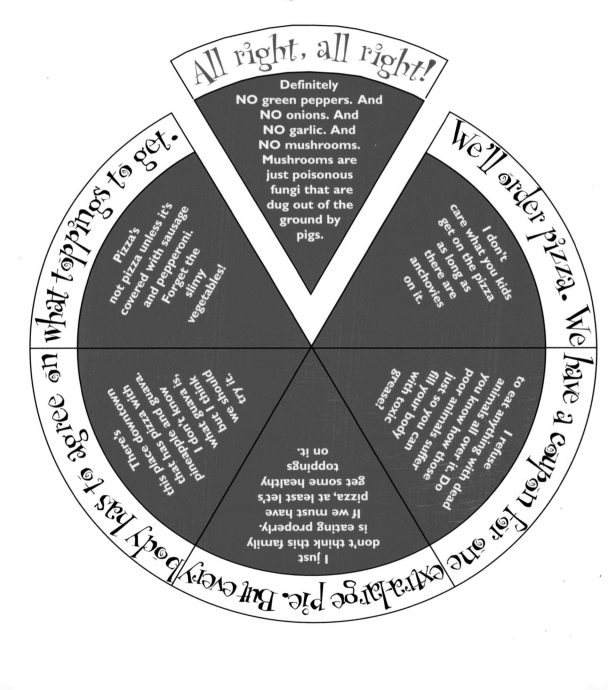

All right, all right!

Definitely **NO** green peppers. And **NO** onions. And **NO** garlic. And **NO** mushrooms. Mushrooms are just poisonous fungi that are dug out of the ground by pigs.

We'll order pizza. We have a coupon for one extra-large pie. But everybody has to agree on what toppings to get.

I don't care what you kids get on the pizza as long as there are anchovies on it.

to eat anything I refuse animals all with dead poor animals over it. Do you know how those just so you can suffer fill your body with toxic grease!

I just don't think this family is eating properly. If we must have pizza, at least let's get some healthy toppings on it.

There's downtown with this place pizza guava. that has and guava. pineapple I don't know what I think but we should try it.

Pizza's not pizza unless it's covered with sausage and pepperoni. Forget the slimy vegetables!

The
Autobiography
of Murray the Fart

I started life as one of the little bubbles in a 16-ounce can of Coke. It was a very happy childhood. I enjoyed playing with all the other little bubbles— my brothers and sisters. Before very long it was time to begin my incredible journey.

Suddenly, we were being sucked through a straw. After a breathtaking ride I found myself in the mouth of a boy

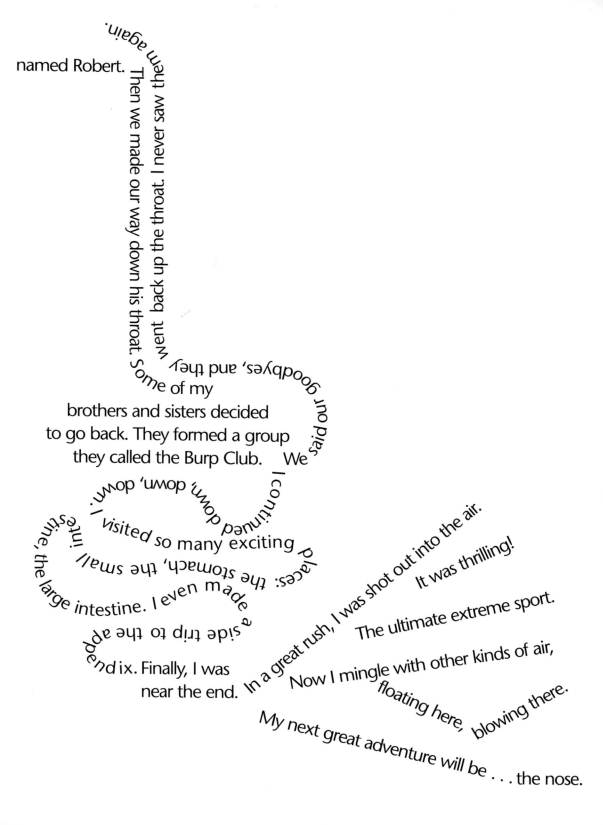

named Robert. ... again.

Then we made our way down his throat. Some of my brothers and sisters decided to go back. They formed a group they called the Burp Club. We said our goodbyes, and they went back up the throat. I never saw them

I continued down, down, down. I visited so many exciting places: the stomach, the small intestine, the large intestine. I even made a side trip to the appendix. Finally, I was near the end. In a great rush, I was shot out into the air. It was thrilling! The ultimate extreme sport. Now I mingle with other kinds of air, floating here, blowing there. My next great adventure will be . . . the nose.

Professional Wrestling for Animals

When an

OCTOPUS (Octopus)

wrestles a

BOA CONSTRICTOR

it's hard to figure out who's winning.

THE LAY-UP

There's a pass across court. Right to me. I'm in the clear. I take off downcourt. Dribbling, running.

A defender blocks me, but I make a little move and get around him. All clear in front of me! Just keep dribbling and don't screw it up.

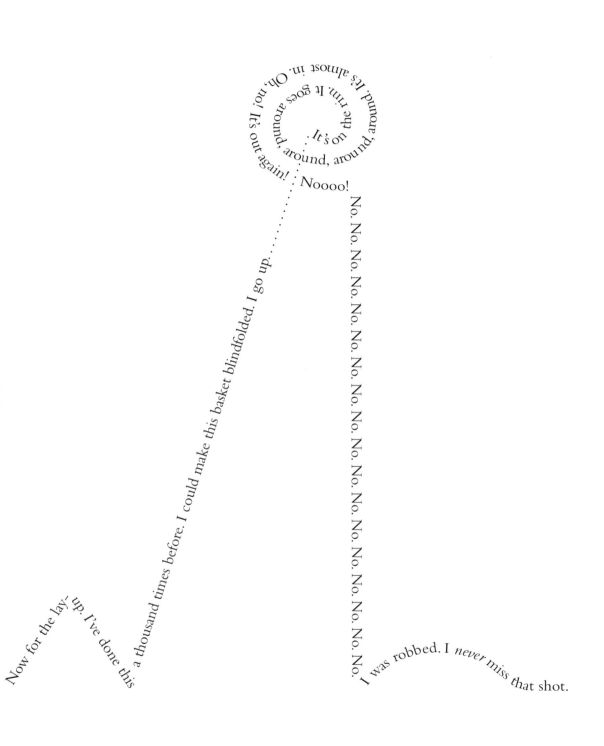

It's on the rim. It goes around, around, It's almost in. Oh, no! It's almost in. around, around, Noooo! It's out again!

Now for the lay- up. I've done this a thousand times before. I could make this basket blindfolded. I go up...

No. No. No. No. No. No. No. No. No. No. No. No. No. No. No. No. No. No. No. No. No. No. No. No. No. No. I was robbed. I *never miss* that shot.

Mom Says, "No New Pets!"

RIP
1998
SSSSAMMY
SSSNEAKY SSSSNAKE

You never should have crawled into the La-Z-Boy

1999
DIGGY
OVERACTIVE HAMSTER
—
HE BROKE HIS NECK IN THE EXERCISE WHEEL

HERE LIES
PIRATE THE CAT
SHE STOLE HER LAST CHICKEN LEG IN 1997

RIZZO
2002
EXCELLENT RAT
CHEWED TO LIVE, LIVED TO CHEW
—BUT NOT THE TOASTER CORD

2000
DIGGY II
YOUR INSIDES FELL OUT YOUR BUTT
—
GROSS!

KNUCKLEHEAD
2004
A PARAKEET WE ALL LOOKED UP TO
—
WATCH OUT FOR CEILING FANS IN HEAVEN

"Why not?"

"The backyard is full."

BLOODCURDLING SCREAMS

My sister makes this cool noise
when she's in the shower
and I flush the toilet.

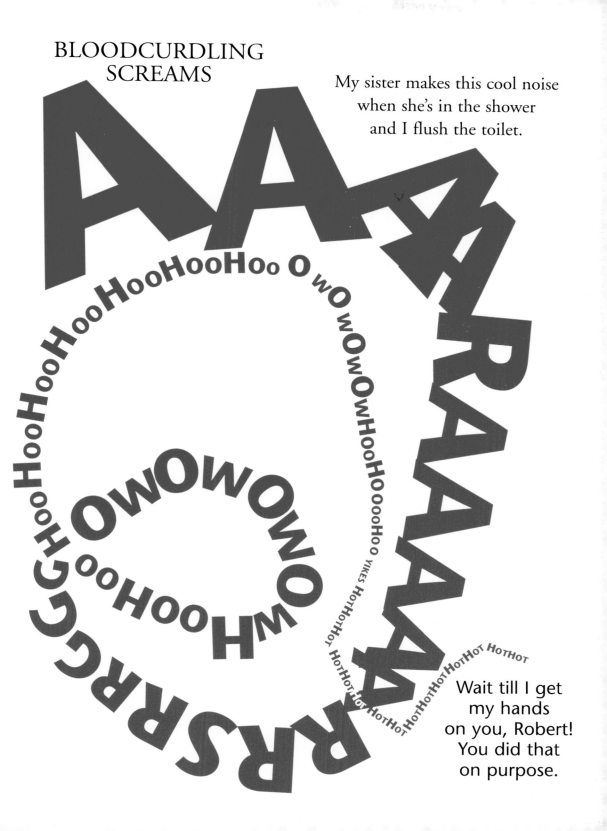

AAAMRAAAAAA

HooHooHooHooHoo O wOwOwHooHooooHoo YIKES HotHotHot
HotHotHotHotHotHot HotHotHotHot HotHot HotHot

GGHooHooHoo OwOwO OwOmOwHOOHoo

RSRRGG RSRRGG

Wait till I get
my hands
on you, Robert!
You did that
on purpose.

Spew Machine

If I designed a roller coaster, you'd really have reason to spew. Of course, I'd have the usual stuff like loop-de-loops. But I'd make them go much faster. Then I'd have you swirling down this slippery drain, around and around until you're so dizzy that you can't even focus. Finally, you'd be in the cannon.

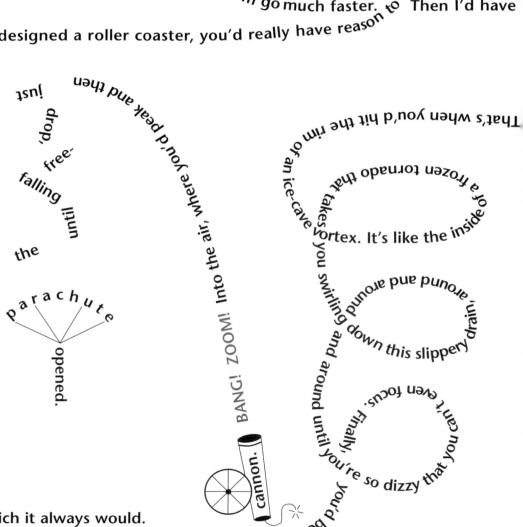

That's when you'd hit the rim of an ice-cave vortex. It's like the inside of a frozen tornado that takes

BANG! ZOOM! Into the air, where you'd peak and then just drop, free-falling until the parachute opened.

Which it always would.
Well, 90% of the time, anyway.

flames shoot out at you when you went by, followed by waves of water in case your clothes caught on fire. The big drop would be really, really steep and really, really long. You'd have to stay upside down and sideways for ages and ages while millions of poisonous killer spiders crawled around your head.

Robert's Four At-Bats

FIRST INNING: Robert hits a long fly ball to deep, deep, deep center field. It looks like it's gonna... He's out!

THIRD INNING: Robert smashes a line drive, but the shortstop

FIFTH INNING: A bouncing ground ball to the second baseman.

BOTTOM OF THE SEVENTH: It's all tied up. Robert comes to bat and

Robert takes off for first. He sees the right fielder boot the ball, so he makes the turn and heads for second. He

out by a step. Shoot!

A wild pitch! Robert breaks for home. It'll be close! He slid-i-i-i-des. SAFE!

tags up and races to third. SAFE!

Cougars win!
Cougars win!
Cougars win!

like it might be out of here! The center fielder goes back, back, back to the fence . . . and makes the catch. Rats!

leaps and makes a fantastic grab. Darn it.

The next batter flies deep to right. Robert

It takes a wicked hop, but he snags it and SAFE!

lines a solid hit

can't see the ball so he sli-i-i-i-i-i-des

to right. The outfielder misjudges the bounce and bobbles the ball.

fires it

over to first. It's close, but Robert is

SICK DAY

When you flush a toilet in the Northern Hemisphere, the water drains in a clockwise direction. They say it goes counterclockwise in the Southern Hemisphere. I try to think about how interesting that is while I'm kneeling here, but all I can think about is the disgusting taste in my mouth.

New Game, Old Computer

Neutrina is totally tough,
totally chill,
totally indestructible.
She enters the Black Cave of Subatomica.

She makes a perfect cliff dive

into the toxic
Muon Marsh.

She jumps from
to   rock
rock   to
rock
across the
Lepton Lava Lake.

She leaps to grab a Pion Vine
in the
Electro-
Rain
Forest.

She swings
in jerky slo-mo
over the abyss
and just freezes.

The little hourglass

flips and flips and flips and
flips and flips and flips.

The computer crashes.
Neutrina is gone—vaporized
into a billion little atoms
scattered someplace
in the hard drive.

Defeated by a
senile computer and
my totally cheap father.

Robert's Bed

I like sleeping over. Your room is so cool.

I will. You've got totally superior stuff.

Let's talk for a while.

How come you always win at chess?

I think it's because you're four years older.

I'm going to practice a lot, and
next time we come to visit, I'll beat you.

I like *Huggin' the Rail*. I can win that game.

Don't be a sore loser.

Great! What?

Okay, I'll start. . . .

. . .

. . .

Hey! No fair.

CONVERSATION

Cousin Paul's Bed

Knock yourself out.

No. I mean it. Knock yourself out—shut up,
be quiet, go to sleep.

You talked all day. You never shut up.
Now go to sleep.

I'm smarter than you.

No, it's because I'm smarter.

I'll still be four years older. And I'll still be smarter.

It's a stupid board game. It's just luck. Whoever
rolls the highest number wins. No skill. All luck.

I have a game we can play.

Who can stay quiet the longest. Ready, set, GO!

. . .

. . .

. . .

It's Not Fair

**Nobody
ever actually
forbid me
to shoot off
fireworks.
Maybe
I should have
known better,
but *technically*
I wasn't disobeying.**

It was cool, though.

The rocket went up very nicely, flying in a graceful arc up over the garage, heading toward

I lit the fuse and watched it burn down.

I'd wrapped my sister's math homework around the tube.

the front yard. Then it exploded,

sparks shooting out

little hunks

in every direction,

of algebra

a tiny star

blasting apart,

going nova,

and then

≥

3

the pieces

∴

y

fluttering

3

>

down

14°

%

2x

+

∞

like

y)

a

(x−

=

42

≤

beautiful

∑

π

x≥

confetti

a+b

parade for

+

∆

9¢

Einstein.

√

I am *so* grounded.
And my parents made me
apologize to my sister.
But it's not *all* bad.
Now she's not talking to me.

Just Mow the Lawn

It doesn't hurt the lawn when you mow it, Robert.
It's just grass.
And that's the lamest excuse you've come up with yet.

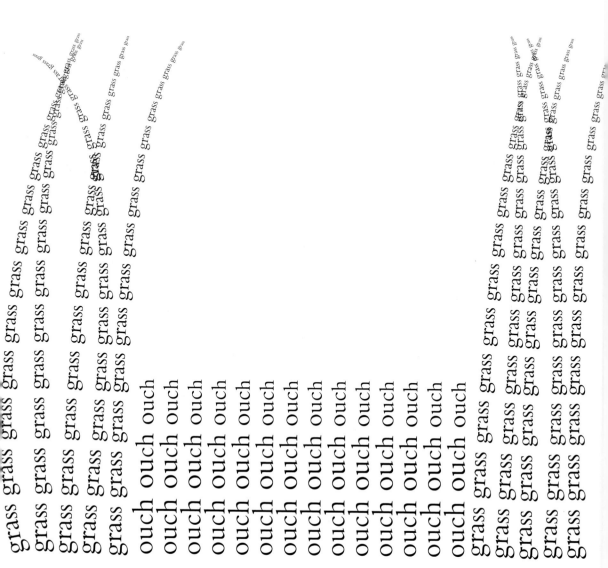

Stop Playing with Your Food!

I ONLY like spaghetti.

It's exactly the same, Robert. Pasta is pasta. By the way, you spelled linguine wrong.

I don't care. It's flat and it's stupid.

Put some tomato sauce on it, you'll never know the difference.

I already know the difference! I'm just going to leave it plain so I can hate it more.

So I've been sitting here for an hour because I have to eat everything on my plate.

THE CAST

I was on my porch when you came down the hill. I never knew a bike could go that fast.
Tommy Z.

I wish I could see the inside of an ambulance! I bet it was great.
Molly S.

I'll bring your homework over every day after school.
XOXO,
Marcia Feddleston

Nice work, bro!
You'd do anything to get out of chores.
Sis

THE
LITTLE
HOUSE

Building
a poem is like
building a little house.
You start
with some bricks—
a pile of words.
They're
all mixed up. There is
no order.
They keep tumbling all over each other.

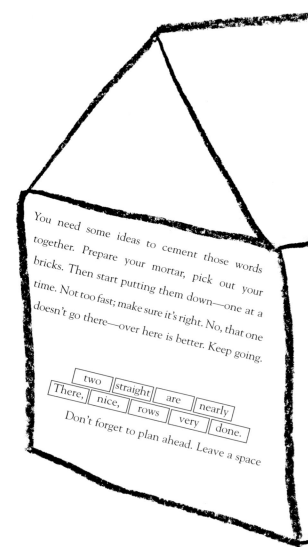

You need some ideas to cement those words together. Prepare your mortar, pick out your bricks. Then start putting them down—one at a time. Not too fast; make sure it's right. No, that one doesn't go there—over here is better. Keep going.

two straight are nearly There, nice, rows very done.

Don't forget to plan ahead. Leave a space